MOUNTAIN MAN'S MATCH

A LONE WOLF'S JOYRIDE TO ROMANCE

VESTA ROMERO

MOUNTAIN MAN'S MATCH

Copyright © 2024 by Vesta Romero

All rights reserved.

CHAPTER 1

*A*lder's hands, calloused and stained, gripped the cool granite before him as he heaved another hefty stone onto the steadily rising wall of his lodge.

The crisp mountain air nipped at his exposed skin while a red-tailed hawk cried out above, slicing through the silence of the Arelis Springs mountains.

He paused, letting the wilderness envelop him, its vastness echoing the hollows in his past.

His lodge provided physical proof of his years of labor and longing for seclusion. He stepped back from it then, surveying his handiwork with pride and a hint of sorrow.

This fortress he had built was not just for protection against the unpredictable elements of the mountain, but also a shield against the memories that haunted him.

As an adventurous teenager, Alder had nearly met his demise while trekking through the same treacherous mountains.

The jagged peaks loomed above him, their icy summits gleaming in the harsh sunlight.

Stranded and alone after becoming separated from his hiking group, he had fought tooth and nail to find his way back to civilization. It was a harrowing experience that stuck with him for years to come.

Decades later, standing at the edge of the very same mountain range, he made the decision to build his own lodge.

It would serve as both a physical sanctuary and a testament to his survival over the unforgiving elements. The sturdy logs were a symbol of his resilience and determination, standing tall against the backdrop of rugged cliffs and verdant forests.

For Alder, the lodge represented so much more than just shelter; it was a tangible reminder of his strength and willpower in the face of adversity.

Alder's gaze drifted over to the small plaque on the side of his lodge, bearing his father's name and the date of completion.

He traced his fingers over the engraved letters, feeling a surge of bittersweet emotions wash over him.

His father had been his rock, his mentor, and his best friend. Together, they had spent countless hours planning and constructing this lodge, pouring their hearts and souls into every detail. Alder had inherited his father's passion for building and it was a legacy that he cherished.

As he gazed out at the peaceful landscape, he was grateful for the bond they'd shared. It was one that had only grown stronger after Alder's mother passed away giving birth to him.

His father had raised him as a single parent, teaching him valuable lessons about life, love, and hard work.

But it wasn't just their shared love for building that brought them together. They had also shared a deep love for nature and all its wonders.

Alder remembered countless camping trips with his father where they would explore new trails and discover hidden gems in the mountains. Those were some of his fondest memories.

Even though his father was no longer with him physically, he could still feel his presence in the lodge they built together. And that thought brought him comfort in times of solitude.

With one last loving glance at the plaque, Alder turned back to his work.

There were still a few finishing touches left to complete before winter set in. There always seemed to be something.

Working tirelessly on those final details, he cherished the memories he carried within in about the lodge that stood as a tribute to both himself and his beloved father.

It took many years of hard work and determination, but he finally had a place where he could escape from the outside world and its constant reminders of what he had lost. Standing there, taking in the beauty of his sanctuary, a sense of peace washed over him.

But even as Alder found refuge in his home against the world, deep down inside he knew that it could never truly erase the pain of his near-death experience. That would always be a part of him, shaping who he was and how he viewed the world.

What was once envisioned as a simple weekend escape quickly became his permanent home as he poured all of his time and resources into turning the lodge into a grand, rustic mountain retreat.

Each addition to the lodge brought with it a deeper sense of belonging and ownership, until it was no longer just a lodge, but a thriving sanctuary nestled in the heart of the rugged mountains. He would continue living within these walls where it was safe and familiar.

With one last look at his lodge, Alder turned and walked back into its protective embrace. For now, it was enough.

Each stone carried a memory, each log was a step further from the world behind him.

CHAPTER 2

*L*ater, nestled by the roaring fire within the half-finished great room, Alder cracked open his laptop, the screen casting an otherworldly glow against the rough-hewn timber.

His fingers danced across the keys, weaving tales of passion and connection that seemed so foreign to his own existence.

He sat back in his leather armchair, staring into the crackling flames of the fireplace.

The half-finished great room was a jumbled mess of materials and tools, but for Alder, it was a sanctuary. A place where he could escape from reality and dive into his own fictional worlds.

With a sardonic smile, he peered into his laptop and began to write. The click-clack of the keys echoed through the quiet lodge as he crafted a scene between two characters that shared a tender, revealing moment.

It was the type of scene that made readers' hearts pulse with desire, a stark contrast to his own isolated life.

As he wrote, Alder couldn't help but think about love which was the one ghost that haunted him most.

It seemed like such a foreign concept to him now, something he could only experience vicariously through his writing.

Continuing to type while letting his imagination run wild, he found himself lost in the world he created on the screen. For those brief moments, it felt like he was living in a different reality. It was one filled with passion and connection.

"Love," Alder mused aloud to the empty room. "You're the one thing I can write about but never quite inhabit."

With a shake of his head, he saved his work and shut his laptop. The click of its closing felt like a door shutting on the world outside, the one that was filled with reminders of what he had lost.

For now, this lodge would remain his protective fort, a place where he could be alone with his thoughts and create stories that allowed him to escape from reality.

Truth be told, reality frightened him and the imaginary world was safer.

The irony wasn't lost on him. The recluse who could ignite loves' fire within the pages of a book while the embers of his own heart lay cold and dormant.

Yet, as the flames flickered and popped in the fireplace, Alder couldn't help but feel a sense of contentment.

Here, in this self-imposed exile, amidst the whispers of pines and the solid earth beneath his feet, he was home.

CHAPTER 3

*T*he next day, Alder stood by the wide, open window of his lodge, staring out at the Arelis Springs mountains that cradled his solitary life.

The cool mountain air carried the scent of pine and earth, a balm to the turmoil that often brewed within him.

Today, he was 45, a milestone that prompted reflection, not celebration. His hands, calloused from years of labor, rested on the worn wood of the windowsill, an indication of a life lived with more substance than sentiment.

He turned away from the view, his gaze falling upon the array of photographs perched on the mantelpiece.

They were snapshots of his past, a visual chronicle of brief companionships with women whose names now echoed faintly in his memory.

None had left an indelible mark; their presence had been like the mist that clung to the mountains, fading, fleeting.

He bent down to stoke the fire, the flames casting dancing shadows across the room.

He had tried the dance of intimacy, stepping into the rhythm with partners not quite suited to his tempo.

The wild oats sown in his youth had grown into nothing more than fields of might-have-beens.

Debra's laughter, though forced, still managed to sparkle in her eyes like scattered rays of sunlight.

Clara, with her eyes constantly fixed on a distant horizon, seemed to long for the bright lights and bustling cities that Alder could never understand.

Each interaction with these women was like adding a vibrant stroke of color onto the otherwise blank canvas of his heart.

His mind wandered to Marianne, the one who had stayed the longest, her stay just shy of nine months. She had moved into his space, filling the silence with music and chatter.

Their nine months together were a cacophony of highs and lows, her presence suffocating yet somehow comforting.

Her vibrancy a stark contrast to the muted tones of his existence. But despite their efforts, they were two notes in a melody that could never harmonize.

The decision to part was mutual, borne of the realization that their union felt more contrived than fated. It was indeed a bitter symphony.

As the last light of day retreated behind the peaks, he picked up a piece of wood, turning it in his hands, feeling the texture under his fingers.

It was solid, real, unyielding, much like the walls he'd built around his heart.

Love was that elusive specter and he had never managed to scale those heights.

Yet, it spilled from his imagination onto the pages of his novels with an intensity that belied his own experiences. Life was funny that way.

It had been many years since Alder had first set foot in the mountains, a young man with big dreams and an even bigger heart.

Somewhere along the way, those dreams faded into the background, replaced by a sobering reality that made him question whether love was worth seeking after all.

He let out a sigh, his gaze sweeping the room once again. There was beauty in simplicity, he knew that now more than ever.

The thought of someone else intruding upon his solitude seemed almost sacrilegious.

But still, there were moments when he longed for the warmth of companionship, for someone to share his home and his life with.

It was a fleeting desire, one that he quickly pushed back down, burying it under layers of practicality and self-preservation.

Alder walked over to the window and gazed out at the breathtaking view once more.

The sun had dipped low by then, painting the sky in shades of soft pink and orange. He wondered if anyone else ever felt as content as he did in this moment.

He had never regretted his decision to isolate himself from society's expectations and norms.

In fact, it had been liberating to live on his own terms, away from the judgement and pressures of others. Or, was it all just a lie to prevent another heartache?

But there was always a small part of him that wondered what could have been if he had chosen differently.

Would he have found love? Would he have been happier? These questions haunted him at times, but ultimately he knew there was no point in dwelling on them.

Alder turned away from the window and headed towards his writing desk. It sat proudly in one corner of the room, surrounded by shelves filled with books and papers scattered randomly around it.

This was where he found solace; where words spilled forth effortlessly onto paper, weaving tales of love and loss that mirrored his own experiences in some ways.

He settled into the familiar seat behind his desk, his fingers traced the well-worn grooves of the polished wood, each imperfection telling a story of years past.

The surface, once smooth and pristine, now bore the marks of countless hours of work and contemplation, memories of stories invented etched into its grain and it made him smile.

CHAPTER 4

*a*aron adjusted his tie with the precision of a man who had mastered the art of looking impeccable, even when the confines of his office no longer held him.

The sun set over Arelis Springs, and it bathed the buildings in a warm golden light that mirrored the ambition and pace that pulsed through the city's veins.

He savored the momentary calm before stepping out into the familiar bustle of evening commuters.

The transition from the concrete jungle to the verdant embrace of the mountains was always marked by a loosening of his shoulders. It was a subtle but tangible shedding of the week's burdens.

As his car climbed the winding road leading away from the town, the skyline in the rearview mirror gave way to the rugged silhouettes of nature's skyscrapers.

Alder greeted him with a nod more telling than any handshake because they were past such formalities.

The mountain air was refreshing, carrying the scent of

pine that seemed to cleanse the remnants of city smog from Aaron's lungs.

Alder led the way to their usual spot, an overhanging cliff that offered a view of the world below, a tapestry of lights flickering like stars come down to earth.

With gloves on, he gripped two icy-cold bottles of beer in his hands, ready to enjoy a laid-back moment.

"Rough week?" Alder asked, his voice steady as the ground they stood on.

"Same old," Aaron replied, but there was a lightness to his words now, buoyed by the openness above and around them.

They talked of small things first, the trivia that filled their days, but it wasn't long before Aaron's news bubbled to the surface, eager to be shared in the quietude that only the mountains could offer.

"Emily and I are getting married," he burst out in a voice laden with happiness.

"Married?" Alder repeated, a grin spreading across his face. "Well, congratulations my friend!"

A wave of relief swept through Aaron as he witnessed Alder's reaction.

Aaron had harbored concerns about how his friend, Alder, would receive the news.

Their longstanding friendship had been rooted in their shared bachelorhood, and Aaron couldn't shake the worry that Alder might react with either dismay or astonishment.

However, as the moment unfolded, Aaron found himself pleasantly surprised.

Rather than encountering any hint of disappointment

or shock, Alder's response overflowed with genuine happiness and support, alleviating Aaron's apprehensions and reinforcing the depth of their bond.

"Yes, it's been a long time coming," Aaron replied, feeling a weight lift off his shoulders. "I've never been happier."

Alder clapped him on the back again before turning to face the expansive view before them.

The city lights twinkled like stars in the distance, reminding Aaron of how far he had come from his small town beginnings.

"I remember when we were just two young kids dreaming of conquering the world," Alder said with a chuckle.

"We did it, didn't we?" Aaron replied with a smile, memories of past travels invading his thoughts.

"We sure did," Alder agreed with a nod. "And now you're taking on your biggest adventure yet. Marriage."

Gazing out at the expansive landscape stretched before them, Aaron couldn't shake a slight sensation of nervousness creeping over him.

He had been confident in his decision to marry Emily, but as he thought about their future together, he couldn't help but wonder what challenges and triumphs awaited them.

But he pushed those thoughts aside for now and turned to face Alder. "Thank you for everything," he said sincerely.

"You know I'll always be here for you," Alder replied with a smile. "Now let's raise our glasses to your future happiness!"

They clinked their bottles together and took in the peacefulness of the moment as they watched the city lights below.

Aaron felt grateful for this friendship that had stood the test of time and was excited for all that lay ahead for him and his soon to be wife.

"Couldn't live without her," Aaron admitted simply, and in those words lay an acknowledgment of love's unpredictable course.

A contrast to the structured life he had built, yet somehow just as essential, just as ingrained to who he was.

It was a statement that held the weight of a thousand rose petals, the soft and fragrant aroma of new beginnings blending with the sharp tang of uncharted territory.

In those words, there was a vulnerability and a strength, a willingness to let go of control and embrace the wild and unpredictable nature of love.

Aaron's admission was like a delicate flower blooming amidst a field of thorns, a reminder that love cannot be tamed or contained, but it is the very essence of what makes us human.

Alder smiled to himself as Aaron's simple sentence that sparked a cascade of vivid imagery in his mind, evoking scenes straight out of a romantic novel.

He made a mental note to treasure this moment and tuck away the phrase for future use in one of his love stories, envisioning how it might beautifully capture the essence of a tender moment between characters.

"The wedding will be an intimate affair, with just close friends and family in attendance," Aaron remarked. He ran his hand through his hair, a small smile tugging at the corners of his lips.

"As expected from you. Is Emily on board with the small guest list?" his friend asked.

Aaron nodded enthusiastically. "Absolutely! In fact, she was more than relieved when I told her." A chuckle escaped him as he remembered their conversation about avoiding a big, elaborate wedding. It seemed they were both on the same page for once about the wedding.

Perched on top of the world, the two buddies basked in the silent comfort of their connection.

Down below, the city lights flickered like distant fireflies, but it was the steady presence of each other that truly anchored them.

For them, words weren't necessary as they soaked in the shared understanding and unwavering support that defined their friendship.

CHAPTER 5

*a*s the morning unfolded, Arelis Springs bathed in the warm glow of sunlight, enveloping the town in a gentle radiance.

The anticipation in the air resonated through the bustling streets, where shadows stretched and danced with the rhythm of the day ahead.

Streams of satin ribbons wove through the streets like an artist's brush, painting the air with vibrant splashes of color.

Bouquets of flowers adorned shop windows, their fragrance mingling with the scent of freshly baked bread and laughter.

"Emily, this place is absolutely enchanting!" Bethany gushed as she stepped off the train, her eyes widening at the sight of the majestic mountains that cradled the town. "I can see why you fell in love with it."

Emily beamed, her cheeks flushed with happiness. "Oh, Beth, I'm so happy you're here! Aaron and I wanted our wedding to be held somewhere special, and Arelis Springs has become our little slice of heaven."

The soon-to-be bride, Emily, had harbored grand visions of her wedding day since she was a little girl, envisioning a celebration filled with all the extravagant trimmings and elaborate details.

From the elegant décor to the lavish floral arrangements, she had meticulously crafted every aspect of her dream ceremony in her mind, yearning for a day that would be nothing short of magical.

But, the more Aaron and her sat together, discussing and refining their plans for the ceremony, it became clear that they both shared a desire for a small, intimate celebration with only close friends and family. It had grown increasingly burdensome and expensive.

Their hands entwined, they knew that their intimate wedding should and would be a retreat of love and cherished moments.

The thought of a grand ceremony filled them with dread, for the chaos and expectations threatened to suffocate their special day.

Only in this small gathering could they truly embrace each other and bask in the pureness of their love. Opting for the smaller wedding was an obvious choice.

As they strolled through the cobblestone streets, Emily filled Bethany in on all the preparations for the big day.

The excitement coursing through the town was palpable; everyone seemed to be pitching in to make sure that the couple's dream wedding became a reality.

"I've never seen anything like this," Bethany admitted,

her urban sensibilities both charmed and slightly over-whelmed by the tight-knit community.

"In the city, people barely know their neighbors, let alone throw a celebration like this for them."

Emily smiled knowingly, a mischievous glint in her eyes. "Just wait until tonight. We're having a pre-wedding bonfire, and the entire town is invited. It's going to be amazing."

Bethany found herself drawn to the untamed beauty of the wilderness that surrounded Arelis Springs as they continued their walk.

The towering mountains seemed to whisper ancient secrets, while the thick forests beckoned her with promises of adventure.

She felt a magnetic pull towards the unknown, as if the mountains were calling her name, but she waved off the sensation as nothing more than a silly notion.

"Emily, I'm not sure how you can bear to be indoors with all this beauty around you," she mused, her gaze lingering on a distant peak.

"Ah, but that's part of the magic," Emily replied, her voice soft and wistful. "Arelis Springs has a way of capturing your heart, and before you know it, you're lost in its embrace."

Bethany couldn't help but agree as they continued their journey through the picturesque town.

The spirit of love and celebration filled the air, and for a moment, she felt as though she had been transported to a different world, one where dreams could come true, and anything was possible.

As the evening of the pre-wedding bonfire unfolded,

Emily's quaint town came alive with the flickering glow of flames and the laughter of friends and neighbors.

It was a gathering of warmth and camaraderie, a celebration of love that transcended the bounds of family ties.

For Bethany, it was a delightful opportunity to meet the townsfolk she had heard so much about.

Surrounded by the welcoming faces and shared stories, Bethany felt a sense of belonging, as if she had found a second home amidst this tight-knit community. Her friend had been lucky to find a wonderful home and she was happy for her.

As the night wore on, under the star-studded sky, bonds were strengthened, and memories were forged.

Bethany longed for a sense of belonging. The desire to belong was a new sensation and one that baffled her.

CHAPTER 6

*E*mily's bachelorette party was in full swing, and she couldn't imagine a more perfect evening.

The backroom of the quaint restaurant had been transformed into a lively dance floor, filled with laughter and chatter.

Bethany danced with her friends, her eyes sparkling with happiness and love for the special people in her life.

Some of the girls she hadn't seen since their old college days, and now, here they were, celebrating together.

"Can you believe I'm getting married tomorrow?" Emily exclaimed as she hugged Bethany tightly.

Bethany grinned from ear to ear, feeling overwhelmed with emotion and so happy for her best friend whom she hugged tightly.

Glasses clinked and music swirled through the open space of the rustic looking backroom of the restaurant. The small circle of friends were having a bachelorette party and basking in the vibrant warmth of friendship and festivity.

Bethany, her cheeks flushed from laughter and the rosy kiss of champagne, danced among her friends, the bride-to-be twirling at her side in a whirl of cream and joy.

The rest of the night flew by in a blur of music, dancing, and heartfelt toasts.

"Let's raise the stakes tonight!" shouted Jenna, her voice slicing through the thumping bass, as she brandished a bottle like a scepter.

The group congregated around her, their movements buoyant, their eyes glistening with mischief under the string lights that crisscrossed the wooden beams above.

"Alright, ladies," Jenna proclaimed with a smirk, "I propose a bet to test our dear Bethany's adventurous spirit since she won't stop yapping on about the fucking mountains!"

Bethany's heart leapt, pulsing in time with the rhythm of the night. She was always one for spontaneity, her life a series of snapshots taken in the thrill of the moment.

This was no different. A grin spread across her face, the allure of the challenge already sending a spark of excitement down her spine.

"Name it," she said, her voice oozing confidence thanks to the drinks.

The circle of friends tightened, each woman's face alight with anticipation.

Jenna's eyes twinkled with playful cunning as she leaned in, lowering her voice to a dramatic whisper.

"If you lose, Bethany, you'll have to spend a full week at Aaron's mountain retreat. Alone and self-sufficient."

An audible gasp rippled through the group, followed by an eruption of giggles and exclamations.

Aaron's cabin was notorious among them, a secluded haven perched high in the mountains, far removed from the bustle and connectivity of their daily lives.

It was both idyllic and intimidating in its isolation.

"Alone?" Bethany echoed, tilting her head to the side. Her thoughts were slightly fuzzy, wrapped in the soft embrace of the evening's indulgences. But the prospect didn't scare her; it intrigued her. "You're on."

"Shake on it!" someone called out.

Bethany reached out, her hand clasping Jenna's firmly, sealing the pact as cheers and hoots encircled them.

Oblivious to the looming silence of the forest or the solitary echo of a cabin bound by nature's whims, Bethany reveled in her decision.

She was not one to back down from a chance to prove herself, least of all on a night designed to celebrate taking risks and diving into life's unknowns.

"May the best woman win," she declared, lifting her glass in toast, the mountain's shadow looming through the window behind her, a silent witness to her bold claim.

The raucous shouts and clinking glasses of a drinking game filled the air.

Bethany, confident in her abilities, stood opposite dear old Sarah, who rarely indulged in alcohol.

The dimly lit room was abuzz with excitement as the two competitors prepared to face off.

Bethany's lips curled into a sly smirk, determined to come out on top. She could practically taste victory in the air, along with the sweet scent of various liquors lingering on her opponents' breath.

The two women raised their glasses and she felt a surge of adrenaline rush through her body, ready for the challenge ahead.

The clink of her glass against another's marked the moment, a seal upon her fate.

Bethany smiled, feeling the weight of the mountains' presence as if they were leaning in to listen.

The raucous laughter of her friends began to fade into the background, the reality of her impulsive decision settling in like the evening mist that crept across the timberline.

As Sarah confidently downed her fifth shot of tequila, Bethany couldn't believe her eyes.

This was the same girl who used to shy away from parties and stick to a single glass of wine.

But here she was, the ultimate champion of the drinking game she had foolishly agreed to play.

The dimmed lights of the restaurant flickered off her triumphant smile as she raised her arms in victory, much to the shock of their group.

How could anyone have predicted that Sarah would become such a wild card, outshining them all with her newfound partying skills?

Needless to say, Bethany lost the bet and Sarah emerged victorious, leaving everyone in disbelief and admiration for her transformation.

"Cheers," she said again, but this time it was softer, introspective. She glanced through the window at the silhouettes of pines standing guard around Aaron's cabin.

The moonlight draped over their tips, silvering edges and deepening the unseen spaces between them.

CHAPTER 7

*B*ethany had always considered herself an adaptive creature, one who could thrive in any setting.

In her mind, she was a chameleon soul with the ability to blend into the vibrant hues of society or the muted tones of solitude.

Yet as the mountain air whispered through a gap in the window frame, carrying with it the scent of earth and pine, she felt a shiver that wasn't entirely due to the night's chill.

"Think of it as just another amazing experience," Jenna said, emerging beside her with a mischievous glint in her eye.

"Or a test of survival skills," Bethany replied, humor lacing her voice even as her heart skipped a beat.

She was not unaccustomed to challenges, but this one held a different flavor, a blend of anticipation and the quiet trepidation of the unknown.

Sensing Bethany's mood, Jenna remarked, "If you want to back out, no one would blame you."

"Absolutely not. I'm sticking with it," Bethany replied firmly.

She turned away from the window, her gaze catching on the fading embers of the fireplace in the back of the room. They glowed like the last whispers of day, promising warmth and then winking out, leaving behind the certainty of a cold and lonely night.

It was a poignant reminder that soon she would be exchanging the comforting buzz of friendship for the stark serenity of nature.

"May your spirit find what it seeks up there," one of the bridesmaids yelled from the back, lifting her own drink in a solemn salute.

"May it be nothing more than peace and quiet," Bethany replied, her laugh tinged with a note of bravado.

She didn't know what awaited her in the embrace of those mountains, but as the party continued around her, the thrill of the impending solitude settled in her bones.

The mountains watched, silent and ancient, as the restaurant flickered with life and laughter.

And in the morning, with the departure of her friends and the arrival of stillness, they would become the stage for an unexpected chapter in Bethany's life.

It would be one that would challenge her resolve, stir her soul, and perhaps redefine her understanding of silence.

It would also set the stage for the next chapter of her life.

CHAPTER 8

*A*t the wedding, Amber's laughter cascaded through the warm evening air, mingling with the twang of country music and the soft shuffling of feet on the dance floor.

Fletch, her husband and partner in all things, including owning the wedding venue where they'd also married, spun her around under the string lights that crisscrossed above the barn's open doors, their joy palpable to every guest.

The onlookers observed the couple with beaming smiles. Once enveloped in sorrow, her journey had led her to Arelis Springs where she found not only love, but also a sense of belonging among its welcoming community.

Alder leaned against the worn wooden railing of the ranch, watching the newlyweds, Aaron and his bride, share a kiss so full of promises you could almost see their future shimmering around them like the fireflies that flickered in the dusk.

The scent of fresh hay and blooming wildflowers was rich in his nostrils as he scanned the crowd, his gaze inevitably drawn to Bethany.

She moved with a grace that belied her voluptuous form, her laughter a melody that seemed to sync with the beat of his own heart.

The lights caught in her hair, framing her face in an amber glow that made it hard for him to look away.

A rush of heat surged through him at the sight of her. His body responded instantly, his cock stirring with desire at the sight of her heavy breasts, their curves and softness calling out to be touched.

The way they moved as she walked was mesmerizing, causing his mind to drift into a haze of desire and longing.

He couldn't help but imagine his hands exploring every inch of her body, his lips trailing kisses along her smooth skin. She was a vision of temptation and he was helpless to resist.

He felt a tightness in his chest, an urgent desire to be closer, to speak to her, but time and opportunity slipped through his fingers like the strands of her hair in the gentle breeze.

When the night drew to a close, the sky exploded in bursts of color from the fireworks, reflecting in Bethany's wide, awe-filled eyes.

Alder's breath caught at the sight, the raw beauty of the moment etching itself into his memory.

He watched her silhouette clap with delight at the rodeo show, the cowboys tipping their hats in the direction of the cheering crowd.

When the time came to send off the couple, a chorus of well-wishes rose up as they drove away to the Leaflee hotel, trailing cans and a 'Just Married' sign.

Alder felt a pang of something like envy, not for the wedding, but for what might have been if he'd had just a little more time with Bethany.

"Tomorrow," he muttered to himself, the resolve settling in his bones. "I'll ask Aaron."

Yeah! On his honeymoon. What guy wouldn't want to talk about another girl while on his honeymoon? Chicken.

But even as he planned, there was an unfamiliar weight to the words, a recognition of the gap between intention and action that seemed wider under the moonlit sky.

With one last glance towards the place where Bethany had stood, Alder turned and headed out into the cool night, the path before him leading back to the solitude of the mountains, where thoughts of curvy silhouettes and missed connections would accompany him until dawn.

CHAPTER 9

*B*ethany's head was pounding, a merciless drumbeat that kept time with her trudging steps as she ascended the winding mountain path.

The brisk air sent a shiver down her spine, the chill nipping at her skin and causing her breath to form small puffs of vapor in front of her.

But the burn in her muscles from the unexpected exertion served as a welcome distraction from the pounding ache in her temples.

She couldn't believe that simply dancing could leave every muscle in her body feeling sore and tired.

The pulsing beat of the music seemed to emanate from the very ground beneath her feet, urging her on to keep moving despite the fatigue that had seeped into her bones.

The thin air at this high altitude took her by surprise, causing her to pause and catch her breath while she drove with the window cracked open.

She wondered if it was simply a product of age, or if the lack of oxygen was truly affecting her.

The corners of her mouth curled into a sly smile as she brushed off the thought and continued on with determination.

She glared at the towering pines, her heart still raw from defeat. The mountains, with their stoic beauty, did little to soothe her ruffled pride.

"Stupid bet," she muttered to herself, as she removed her small suitcase from the trunk of her car once she'd located the cabin.

The suitcase she had brought along seemed comically out of place for the week ahead.

It was a luxurious leather case, packed to the brim with delicate silk blouses and elegant high heels, items utterly mismatched for the rugged terrain that lay before her.

Yet, as she surveyed the wild expanse of the wilderness she now found herself in, she chuckled at the irony of her situation. After all, she hadn't anticipated embarking on a week-long adventure in the woods when she initially packed for the wedding she had come to attend.

Once inside the cabin, a rustic abode of timber and stone that seemed to mock her with its masculine austerity, Bethany surveyed the room with distaste.

Her nose wrinkled at the sight of mounted antlers and well-worn leather furniture, further adding to the overall ruggedness of the place.

A shiver ran down her spine; it wasn't just the lack of warmth that unsettled her, but the overwhelming silence, pressing against her ears like an unwelcome guest.

She took a deep breath, trying to calm herself as she reminded herself that this was only temporary.

She was here for a purpose which was to prove that she could handle anything the other women threw at her. If that meant spending a few days in a remote cabin in the mountains, then so be it.

Looking around at the cold and uninviting space, she acknowledged feeling a twinge of regret for agreeing to this bet in the first place.

What had started off as a playful challenge had turned into something much more intimidating once Bethany saw what she was up against.

The elements! Now, she was stuck in this isolated wilderness with no escape and she wasn't willing to give the girls satisfaction.

Stubborn mule!

With a sigh, Bethany made her way towards one of the large windows overlooking the vast expanse of trees outside. She leaned against the wooden frame, taking in the breathtaking view while also trying to compose herself.

As much as she wanted to be stubborn, she knew deep down that she should admit defeat and leave.

Bethany shook her head, chastising herself for even entertaining such thoughts. She didn't need anyone's help. She could do this on her own.

But as night began to fall, silhouetting the trees against a fiery sky, Bethany felt her first rush of fear.

"Great," she sighed, realizing the fire had long since died in the stove, leaving behind cold ashes.

Her city life had never required her to wield an axe, let alone saw wood, but here, there was no room service to call, no thermostat to adjust. She stepped outside into the chill, squaring her shoulders against the task ahead.

She picked up a log, placed it on the stump doubling as a chopping block, and took a heavy swing with the axe. The blade glanced off the wood, sending a jolt up her arms.

"Dammit!" she cursed aloud, feeling the sting of incompetence. Again and again, she swung, each miss igniting a fresh spark of anger within her.

Defeated by the stubborn log, she stormed into the storage room, rummaging through shelves until her fingers curled around the handle of an old chainsaw.

Pulling the cord with more hope than skill, she winced at the coughing sputter of the engine refusing to turn over.

Her frustration erupted into a string of expletives so vivid and explicit, they would make even the most hardened sailor blush.

Each curse was like a fiery burst of emotion, punctuated with fierce gestures and flailing arms.

The words seemed to physically escape her mouth, swirling around her like a raging storm. They were sharp and precise, each one hitting its mark with ferocious accuracy.

It was as if she were using them as weapons, channeling all of her pent-up anger and disappointment into an explosive verbal assault.

By the end of her tirade, she was left trembling and breathless, but somehow satisfied in release.

CHAPTER 10

*U*nbeknownst to Bethany, the commotion sliced through the tranquil mountain air like a sharp knife.

The stillness of the surrounding peaks was broken by the echoes of shouting and rustling, finding its way to the ears of Alder, who lived just a ridge away in his own secluded haven.

With a furrowed brow and curious mind, he left his peaceful abode to investigate the disturbance at what should have been an empty cabin since Aaron was on his honeymoon.

His steps were heavy with anticipation as he made his way towards the source of the commotion, unsure of what he would find when he arrived.

Upon his approach, his gaze was captured by the delicate curve of her hips as she bent over the chain-saw, her body moving in a graceful yet powerful rhythm.

Strands of hair, wild and untamed, fell in disarray

around her face, framing features that were both striking and alluring.

Recognition slowly dawned on him and his mouth dropped open in disbelief. It was her, the enigmatic woman from the wedding the day before whose image had lingered in his thoughts.

She was there, cursing at machinery in the middle of his peaceful surroundings. The contrast between her presence and the tranquil scenery was jarring, yet somehow fitting for this mysterious woman who seemed to possess a raw magnetism that drew him in.

A small smile tugged at the corners of Alder's mouth as he leaned against the sturdy wooden frame of the door, fully engrossed in watching her futile attempts to start the stubborn saw.

His initial irritation had long since dissolved, replaced by a warm amusement that only grew with every pull of the cord and every inventive curse that escaped her lips.

"Need some help?" he finally called out, unable to contain his deep chuckle at the sight before him.

The sun glinted off of the metallic surface of the saw, and it cast intricate patterns of light and shadow across the grassy meadow.

The smell of fresh, grisly cut wood lingered in the air, mingling with the subtle scent of wildflowers.

Alder felt a curious a sense of peace wash over him as he watched her struggle, knowing that he would soon be able to offer his assistance.

Bethany whipped around, eyes blazing, the chainsaw forgotten in her hands as she met the gaze of her uninvited audience.

Her cheeks flushed a deeper red, not from the cold, but from a cocktail of embarrassment and rising ire at his obvious entertainment at her expense.

A fiery heat ignited between her thighs, leaving her body trembling and aching with desire.

The enigmatic stranger had her twisted in knots of need, trapped in a web of intoxicating attraction that she couldn't and didn't want to escape from.

The man's voice cracked as he sheepishly asked, "Do you remember me from the wedding?"

Her response was sharp and swift, tinged with a hint of desire. "I would have remembered if I had met you," she replied quickly, her cheeks flushing a deep shade of red in embarrassment.

That was much too quick

"Oh, you probably had too much to think about," there was noticeable disappointment in his tone.

A gust of wind rustled the leaves, causing Bethany to shiver involuntarily. She wrapped her arms around herself, trying to preserve what little warmth she had left.

Alder noticed her discomfort and raised an eyebrow inquisitively.

"I live in the next lodge," he offered in explanation.

"Hard to believe someone would willingly come up here and live in this cabin," Bethany mused aloud, attempting to distract herself from the chill. "I mean, the city is just a short drive away, with all its comforts."

"True," Alder admitted, his gaze following a few stray leaves as they danced in the breeze. "But I've found that living off the grid like this has its own unique appeal. It's an acquired taste, really."

Bethany eyed him curiously, intrigued by the notion of someone choosing that lifestyle over the familiar hustle and bustle of the city. "How did you come to acquire it, then?" she asked.

Alder chuckled softly, remembering the first days he spent in the cabin. "Well, it took some time getting used to the solitude and simplicity. But eventually, I grew to appreciate the quiet moments and the beauty of nature that surrounds us."

As another gust of wind swept through, Bethany's teeth chattered, and Alder noticed her obvious discomfort. Her nipples were visible even through her light sweater. Feeling a surge of sympathy for her plight, he offered a solution:

"Would you like to come over to my place for some coffee? To warm you up, I mean," he added quickly, hoping not to sound too forward.

At first, Bethany hesitated, torn between the desire for warmth and her promise to be self-sufficient during her stay at the cabin.

Then again, she rationalized, accepting a cup of coffee could hardly be considered cheating, right?

"Alright," she conceded with a grateful smile. "A cup of coffee sounds lovely, thank you."

"Great," Alder beamed. "My place is just a short walk from here."

CHAPTER 11

Strolling through the woods during their short distance, Bethany found herself questioning her initial skepticism about living in the wilderness.

Perhaps there was some merit to Alder's perspective after all, an acquired taste she might even come to enjoy.

When Alder walked towards her, she had noticed his broad shoulders and chiseled jawline.

He exuded an aura of confidence and charm that reminded her of the heroes in her romance novels.

She felt a surge of attraction wash over her, causing her pulse to quicken and her cheeks to flush.

As they approached the cabin, Bethany couldn't help but stare at Alder's back, admiring the way his muscles moved under his shirt.

She had envisioned a rugged, grizzly, mountain man straight out of a film, living in solitary seclusion.

However, upon meeting Alder, she was pleasantly surprised. His beard, though short, was meticulously groomed, and his dark hair, just beginning to show hints of gray at the sides, framed his handsome features.

Standing tall, he exuded a sense of confidence and allure that caught her off guard.

As she observed him, a small smile tugged at the corners of her lips. He was indeed a tall drink of water, as the saying went, and the combination of his appearance and demeanor was undeniably attractive.

Alder unlocked the door and held it open for her, gesturing for her to enter first. Bethany stepped inside and immediately felt the warmth from the crackling fire in the stone fireplace.

The cabin was cozy and rustic, with wooden beams and furniture that seemed to fit perfectly into the natural surroundings.

"Make yourself comfortable," Alder said as he walked over to the kitchen area. "I'll just put on some coffee."

Bethany took off her coat and hung it on a nearby hook before taking a seat on one of the plush armchairs by the fire.

She crossed her legs and wrapped her arms around herself, trying to warm up from the inside out.

Alder returned with two steaming mugs of coffee and handed one to Bethany before taking a seat across from her. For a moment, they sat in silence, sipping their coffee and enjoying its warmth.

"I have to admit," Bethany finally broke the silence. "This place is quite charming."

Alder smiled at her remark. "It's definitely not for everyone," he replied. "But I'm glad you appreciate it."

They chatted about various topics, starting with the

weather, their hobbies, and other small talk as they finished their coffee.

The more they talked, the more Bethany found herself drawn to Alder's easygoing demeanor and sense of humor.

After she finished her coffee, Alder kindly extended an offer to give her a tour of his cabin, beginning with the bedroom situated on the second floor.

Surprisingly, she didn't find his suggestion odd in the least. Perhaps it was the casual and genuine manner in which he proposed it, or maybe it was the natural ease of their conversation that made such an invitation feel perfectly normal.

Whatever the reason, she accepted without hesitation, curious to explore more of his cozy abode and learn about the man who inhabited it.

"This is my favorite spot," he said as he opened the door to a room with a large window overlooking the vast expanse of the mountains.

The setting sun flooded the room with a gentle, amber hue, enveloping every object in its soothing warmth. Bethany gasped at the breathtaking view and knew then why he had chosen to start with the best.

The snow-capped peaks stretched out before her like a majestic painting, their rugged beauty making her heart skip a beat. It felt as if she could reach out and touch the stars that scattered across the darkening sky.

"Wow," she whispered, her voice filled with awe. "This is absolutely stunning."

Alder grinned, his eyes twinkling with a mixture of

pride and joy. "I'm glad you think so," he said softly. "This view never ceases to amaze me."

Bethany turned to face him, her eyes wide with wonder. There was something outstanding about the place, she realized, something that stirred her soul and ignited a sense of adventure within her.

"I don't think I've ever experienced anything like this before," she admitted, her voice barely above a whisper. "Being here, it makes me feel alive."

Alder's smile grew wider, his gaze filled with understanding as words of his father appeared to him. "Nature has a way of doing that," he replied, his voice gentle yet filled with conviction. "It reminds us of the wonders and beauty that exist beyond our everyday lives."

They stood there, side by side, gazing out at the panorama before them, an unspoken connection forming from a shared appreciation for the serenity and magnificence of nature's embrace.

With a deliberate yet tender gesture, Alder extended his hand, intertwining his fingers with Bethany's in a slow and deliberate manner.

To his delight, she didn't pull away; instead, she welcomed the connection, finding it to be an instinctive and comforting gesture.

What pleased him even more was her ability to recognize and admire the beauty around them, a quality he deeply admired in her.

CHAPTER 12

*B*ethany cradled the warm mug between her hands, the remnants of their coffee date cooling with each passing moment. She'd accepted a second cup.

She watched Alder with a gentle curiosity that danced in her eyes, a soft smile gracing her lips as he recounted yet another tale from his global escapades with Aaron.

The stories unfurled like vivid collages, each one woven with the kind of authenticity that made it clear why their mutual friend had found love so easily.

Alder's laughter was infectious, his gestures grand as he described navigating through crowded streets and serene landscapes alike.

"Can you believe Aaron almost married a street performer in Prague?" Alder quipped, his eyes alight with mischief.

"Really?" Bethany chuckled, tilting her head with genuine interest. "He never struck me as the impulsive type."

"Ah, but that's the thing about travel and drink," Alder mused, his gaze drifting to a memory only he could see. "It peels back the layers, shows you who you really are."

Bethany's heart raced quietly in her chest, an unspoken thought lingering in her mind.

What layers would be peeled back if she and Alder were to embark on such a journey together? But she brushed the idea away, content for now with the comfortable ebb and flow of their conversation.

As she observed him, she noticed the lack of any traces of a significant other in his life.

There were no framed pictures on his desk or scattered throughout his apartment, no mention of a partner in casual conversation.

It was as if he existed solely in this moment with her, uninterrupted by any outside relationships.

The realization brought a subtle blush to her cheeks and a flutter of hope in her stomach.

She refrained from prying, knowing it wasn't her place, but the curious thought lingered in her mind like a delicate flower waiting to bloom.

Meanwhile, Alder observed the slender curve of her fingers around the mug, the lack of adornment on her left hand. It meant little, perhaps nothing at all, but curiosity gnawed at him.

He edged around the topic, questions camouflaged in casual anecdotes and inquiries about her work, her hobbies, until she answered his unasked question.

"I'm not seeing anyone, if that's what you're trying to ask," Bethany blurted, a mix of embarrassment and cheekiness washing over her.

She averted her gaze, focusing on a stray coffee bean on the table. "I'm 36 and still single and I sometimes feel like I'm destined to become an old maid." It was the first time she had voiced it out loud.

Alder's voice quivered with emotion as he spoke, his hand trembling as it reached across the table to gently cover Bethany's own. "Old maid? That's preposterous. I don't think anyone is destined to be anything," he said gently, "Life has a funny way of surprising us. You're so much more than that, Bethany. You're extraordinary in every way from what little I've seen." His words hung in the air, heavy with adoration.

"I believe there's someone out there for everyone," Alder continued sincerely. "It's just a matter of timing and being open to it. Besides, I'm 45 and still single. So there. You're not alone!"

"45? You don't look a day over 35." Her words dripped with sincerity as she gazed at him, taking in every chiseled feature of his face.

He was the epitome of tall, dark, and handsome. To her, he was more like a Greek god come to life, radiating raw masculinity and rugged attractiveness. He shattered her expectations

"Newly minted one too. In fact, I celebrated with Aaron just days before his wedding."

"Happy belated birthday then. There's hope for us yet then."

Bethany's blush deepened as she absorbed Alder's words, a tinge of uncertainty creeping into her mind.

She had never been one to seek out flattery, and yet,

his genuine admiration made her feel something she couldn't quite put a name to.

"Thank you," she managed to say with a shy smile, pulling her hand away to adjust her glasses nervously. "But I think you're biased."

"Oh, no my dear," Alder chuckled, leaning back in his chair and crossing his arms over his chest. "I'm quite certain that anyone who meets you would come to the same conclusion."

Bethany's heart skipped a beat at the thought of anyone else seeing her in the same light as Alder did. It was a foreign sensation, one she wasn't sure how to handle.

Their conversation eventually drifted away from their mutual friend and onto other topics, books they'd read, movies they'd seen, and places they'd traveled.

Each new revelation only added to their growing connection, their shared interests building an unbreakable bond between them.

Their eyes met, a silent understanding passing between them. In that instant, the shy banter and unspoken thoughts gave way to an evolving connection, fragile yet filled with possibilities.

CHAPTER 13

*B*ethany glanced at the elongated shadows across Alder's porch. With a start, she realized hours had passed in his company, hours that were filled with laughter and an easy camaraderie she had not anticipated finding here, on this solitary mountain.

"I better get going," she murmured, rising suddenly but with a hint of reluctance, causing the wooden chair to scrape against the floorboards.

Alder rose as well, concern knitting his brow. "Can I help you with the woodpile before you head back?" he offered, gesturing to the ax leaning against the wall.

"Thanks, but no," Bethany replied, her voice firm despite the fluttering in her chest. "I made a bet. I have to do this on my own."

The realization washed over her then and she felt a pang of embarrassment at her oversight.

The empty cupboards and bare shelves in Aaron's cabin were a stark reminder of her lack of preparation.

She had ventured into the wilderness without even considering the basics of sustenance.

It was a humbling moment, one that made her question her readiness for the rugged lifestyle of a mountaineer.

The thought of descending the mountain's treacherous paths again in the darkness made her stomach twist uncomfortably, but her stomach was growling. She cursed herself for being so foolish and not planning ahead.

"Hey," Alder called out as if reading her mind, reaching into a cupboard. "Take this." He extended a can of tuna and a packet of crackers toward her. She'd told him about the foolish bet and he knew she wouldn't accept anything more.

"Are you sure?" Her brows furrowed, torn between pride and practicality.

"Of course," he smiled. "I don't think this little will count against you in your contest, will it?."

"I don't think so either. Besides, how can I win if l die of starvation?" she said with a laugh as she accepted the food. A warm feeling spread through her as their hands touched briefly.

"Let me walk you back," Alder insisted, grabbing a couple of blankets from a chest by the door. "It gets cold fast after dark," he teased, his eyes crinkling in amusement.

"Thanks," Bethany mumbled, feeling a blush creep up her cheeks. She welcomed the warmth of the blankets draped over her arm, a surrogate for the comfort his presence provided.

They walked side by side in companionable silence,

the forest around them hushing as if to respect their solitude.

When they reached the clearing where Bethany's cabin stood, the moment stretched taut between them.

"Here we are," Alder said, his voice low.

"Here we are," Bethany echoed, her heart pounding in her ears.

They stood facing each other, the air charged with unspoken words and desires not acted upon.

Their eyes met, held, and something flickered there, a question, a possibility. Yet neither moved closer.

"Goodnight, Bethany," Alder finally whispered, the words hanging heavy in the cool night air.

"Goodnight, Alder," she responded, equally hushed.

With one last lingering look, they parted ways, the space between them widening with each step.

No kiss was exchanged, only the silent promise of what could be, left floating like dandelion seeds on the mountain breeze.

Chickens!

CHAPTER 14

*B*ack in the cabin, Bethany slumped into an old armchair, its cushions long past their prime, and sighed in frustration.

With no television to occupy the rest of the night, she begrudgingly chastised herself for not bringing any reading material.

"God, I can't believe there isn't even a TV here," she muttered under her breath. Her eyes scanned the room, searching for something, anything, that might offer a semblance of entertainment.

To her surprise, she discovered a small stash of books tucked away behind the couch, dust-laden and seemingly untouched for years.

Bethany's eyebrows shot up at the sight of the sultry covers. They were not just any books, but spicy romantic novels.

Curiosity piqued, she plucked one from the pile and began reading, quickly becoming engrossed in the passionate tale.

Her heart raced as the protagonist, a dashing man with dark hair and piercing eyes, reminded her of Alder, the brooding neighbor she had met earlier.

'Wouldn't it be fun to write something like this myself? It sounds a lot better than the over the top romantic ones that I write" she thought, but the heat building within her made it impossible to concentrate on anything other than her own arousal.

A shower seemed like the best solution to cool off, so she stripped down, determined to let the cold water cascade over her body and cool her off, but despite her efforts, the thoughts of Alder continued to consume her, leaving her restless and unsatisfied.

Her resolve finally overpowered her fear and she whispered to herself, "Enough is enough."

With shaking hands, she peeled off her clothes and searched through Aaron's mudroom for the largest jacket available. It hung heavily on her frame as she slipped it on, along with her sturdy boots, the only sensible thing she'd brought on her trip.

The cold gusts of the night air nipped at her skin, raising goosebumps and sending shivers down her spine.

Taking a deep breath to steady herself, she stepped outside into the darkness, heart pounding with a mix of anticipation and nerves like a drumbeat in her chest.

"Come on, Bethany, you can do this," she murmured, offering herself a final pep talk before striding toward Alder's cabin.

Each step felt heavier than the last, but she refused to back down. At last, she arrived at his door and took a deep breath.

With courage she didn't know she possessed, Bethany raised her hand and knocked loudly, sealing her fate with every reverberating echo.

CHAPTER 15

*R*estless energy thrummed through Alder's veins as he tossed another balled-up attempt at writing into the trash bin.

The blank page on his screen was as empty as the hollow ache within him, an ache that had a name. Bethany.

He slouched in the chair, his gaze flitting toward the silent television. Images danced and flickered, but they were just shadows; Bethany's silhouette haunted the edges of his vision.

He rose, pacing the floorboards that creaked under the weight of his unrest. Through the window, he peered into the darkness towards where her cabin lay among the trees. Was she awake? Did her thoughts reach out to him, tangling with his in the night air?

With a heavy sigh, Alder collapsed onto the edge of his bed, feeling the press of indecision. He went out determined to call on her.

Footsteps halfway to her cabin where she probably

fast asleep with no thought of him, then retreating. It was a dance of hesitation. Love or lust? Connection or carnal desire?

The questions tormented him, pulling at the frayed edges of his solitude.

He extinguished the lights, surrendering to the enveloping gloom. The darkness caressed his skin like an intimate whisper, promising solitary release from the torment of his longing. He reached for the warmth of his own touch, seeking solace.

A sudden, urgent pounding shattered the stillness. His heart leapt. Bethany! Panic and desire surged as one, propelling him to the door. He fumbled with the latch, throwing it open with a force born of fear and yearning.

The night breeze carried a chill, but none so cold as the sight that greeted him.

There stood Bethany, vulnerable and ethereal, the oversized coat falling open to reveal her nakedness, her skin a canvas of moonlight. Strands of hair escaped her bun, wreathing her face with a halo of disarray. Her lips parted, trembling with audacity and need.

"I'm cold. Can you help?" Her voice was a breath, a dare, an invocation.

Oh, could he! All the answers he sought seemed to crystallize in that single moment of raw honesty between them.

CHAPTER 16

*A*lders' senses were assaulted by the heady perfume of raw desire as his gaze feasted upon the voluptuous vision before him.

Her silhouette was a siren's call, curves etched with an artist's precision, culminating in the bold declaration of her femininity.

The sight sent waves of heat coursing through his veins, his pupils dilating with rapt attention.

"I couldn't stay away," Bethany said softly, her eyes searching his for any sign of rejection.

But all Alder saw was truth and longing in those deep green eyes. Without hesitation, he closed the distance between them and captured her lips with his own.

The kiss was fierce and desperate at first, each trying to convey all their unspoken emotions through their touch.

Every touch of her lips and tongue was like a sweet and addictive nectar, igniting his taste buds and driving him wild with desire.

The way she teased and tantalized his body with her mouth was a taste he could never get enough of.

The taste of her lips and tongue was like a heady intoxication, the sweetness of her mouth mingling with his own salty taste as she explored him with a skilled passion.

They continued to explore each other's mouths with a hunger that bordered on desperation, their kiss turned into something more, a promise of passion and connection that surpassed any words they could have spoken.

When they finally pulled away for air, Bethany rested her forehead against Alder's chest and whispered,

"I've been wanting this since the moment I met you."

"You have no idea how long I've waited for you," Alder replied hoarsely.

And then they were kissing again, their hands roaming over each other's bodies as if trying to memorize every curve and dip. Alder's mind was a blur of sensations, his heart pounding so hard he thought it would shatter and splinter within his body.

With a surge of primal urge, Alder's arms encircled the softness of her waist, and he hoisted her into the air as if she were no more than a breath.

A symphony of giggles danced in the air as they crossed the threshold of sanctuary, his bedroom, where inhibitions were left to starve at the door.

His lips found their prize, latching onto the tender peak of her breast, eliciting from her a melody of playful laughter that stoked the fire within him.

Her jacket which was a mere bystander to their fervor, slid from her shoulders like the final barrier to their carnal communion, and with gentle reverence, Alder laid her upon the bed, the altar of his impending worship.

In a dance as old as time, his own garments fell away, piece by discarded piece, revealing the hunger etched in every line of his body.

His arousal stood as a monument to their mutual craving, and her eyes, glinting with a predator's anticipation, drank in the sight.

As he enveloped her with his presence, their mouths collided, a conflagration of tongues and teeth, each kiss with an urgency that pulsed between them.

Their bodies entangled in a frenzy of passion, limbs twisting and sheets tangling as they exchanged positions.

With a boldness fueled by desire, she took control, her hands claiming ownership of his throbbing cock.

Her voice, thick with lust, commanded him onto his back with a primal urgency. "I want all of you," she breathed, her words dripping with irresistible promises of unbridled pleasure that sent shivers down his spine.

Her lips were parted and glistening with anticipation as she descended upon him, her movements fluid and graceful like a dancer's.

Her skilled hands and fingers expertly caressed every inch of his body, igniting a fire within him.

Her head bowed down, cascading locks of hair blocking his view but allowing him to focus on the movement of her lips, the arch of her back, and the fluidity of her motions.

Her eyes, locked on his face, glistened with passion and her skin flushed with desire.

Her head dipped downward, her long hair a curtain of

silk cascading over his chest and abdominal muscles as she descended towards her destination.

Her movements were fluid and graceful, almost like a dance as she expertly explored every inch of his body.

With each movement, he could feel the heat of her mouth and the softness of her lips against his skin. Her hands, exploring and caressing every inch of his body, sent shivers of pleasure through him.

Her lips and tongue were like fire on his skin, each touch sending sparks of pleasure throughout his body. Her fingers traced patterns along his chest and stomach, igniting each nerve with electric sensations.

Nothing was left untouched as she eagerly explored every inch of his body with her skilled hands.

From the throbbing ache in his balls to the sensitive skin of his shaft, and even the most intimate areas, she showered him with an intense and unending focus as she sucked and licked, sending electric shivers down his spine. Her mouth seemed tailor made for his cock and he thrust upward enthusiastically.

Every touch was deliberate and purposeful, her hands were everywhere and moved with practiced precision that drove him wild.

The sensation of her warm breath on his skin only heightened the pleasure, making him feel like he was being consumed by desire.

He could feel every nerve in his body light up as she explored every inch of him, leaving no corner untouched. It was an exquisite torture, but one that he never wanted to end.

Alder was lost, spiraling in a whirlpool of sensation, each stroke of her tongue pushing him closer to the edge.

As the moment of release approached, it built within him like a raging storm, thundering and crashing against his body.

When it finally came, it was like a monumental force, shattering through every fiber of his being with the intensity of a tidal wave.

His semen flowed forth, a sacred offering to be consumed by his devout disciple.

She received it with fervent devotion, savoring its taste as though she had been blessed by the divine itself and he had never been prouder. The air around them seemed to hum with an otherworldly energy as they were consumed by this ritual of passion and worship.

They purred with satiation at the aftermath, their heavy breaths evidence of the storm that had raged moments before.

As her lips pressed against his, he could feel his body ignite with a fierce desire that consumed every inch of him.

He was desired like never before, and it sent his mind spiraling into a frenzy of passion and longing.

CHAPTER 17

*A*lder lay there, a sheen of perspiration covering his body like morning dew on grass, the after-glow of pleasure still flickering in his eyes.

The room was thick with the scent of their union, a tangible reminder of the fervor that had consumed them both.

As he regained his senses, he felt her soft lips press against his own, tender yet insistent. In that intimate exchange, he tasted the salty-sweet flavor of himself, an erotic signature left upon her tongue.

Her kiss was deep, drawing him back to the present, back to the unquenchable need for her that simmered within him.

With a sudden surge of desire, Alder acted. His hands, those skilled and knowing instruments, sought out the warmth between her thighs.

Her breath caught as his fingers slipped into her, teasing her velvety depths with a lover's knowledge.

He whispered praise and promises into her ear, each word a delicate brushstroke on the canvas of her arousal.

His thumb mercilessly pressed against her pulsing clit, sending shockwaves of pleasure through her body like a maestro conducting his masterpiece.

Her hips bucked in rhythm to his touch, each moan a note in the symphony of their passion.

As he plunged two of his fingers deep inside her, she let out a guttural cry that reverberated through the room.

The sensation was overwhelming, intense waves of pleasure crashing over her as he worked his fingers in and out with expert precision. She arched her back, bucking against him, lost in a state of pure euphoria.

He played her body like a virtuoso, his fingers moving in a frenzy as she reached the peak of ecstasy.

The climax, when it arrived, was a powerful wave that crashed over her, leaving her drenched in the ecstasy of release. Her essence coated his hand, proof of the intensity of her pleasure.

They paused, a momentary lull in the tempest of their desire, catching their breaths as the reality of their hunger for one another settled around them like a cloak.

Her body, flushed with desire, quivers as he positions her on her knees on the bed.

His hands move down her curves, spreading her wider as his thumbs part her slick, glistening pussy lips.

His thumbs on her folds were gentle yet skilled, eliciting moans and shivers from her body.

She had a small landing strip of hair, barely visible against the smooth skin of her mound.

He positioned himself over her, his stiff cock glistening with the wetness of their arousal, and in one swift movement, buried himself inside her. Her juices coated his cock, adding to the intense and primal flavor.

His hands on her hips were firm and strong, guiding and holding her in place. She felt him inside her, thick and hard, filling her completely.

He delved deep and found her core, their bodies melding together in a primal and passionate dance.

The room was filled with the intoxicating fragrance of their desire, igniting Alder's senses and driving him further into a frenzy.

Their bodies, slick with sweat and flushed with desire, moved in a primal rhythm.

Alder's fingers gripped her hips tightly, leaving red marks on her skin as he marked her as his own. She arched her back, her eyes glazed over with pleasure, meeting his powerful thrusts.

Their bodies, slick with sweat and flushed with desire, moved together in perfect harmony.

The muscles in his arms flexed with each powerful thrust, while her body arched to meet him, her curves highlighted by the soft candlelight.

Their bodies entwined in a frenzy of passion, skin flushed and glistening with sweat. Her hair was wild and tangled, framing her flushed and blissful face.

Alder's hands gripped her hips possessively, fucking smoothly and sometimes reaching around to grab her plump breasts in his hands.

She delighted at the sensation of his balls slapping against her thighs as she swallowed all of his thick member in her pussy. She reached down to cup them in her palms, gently rubbing as she egged him on.

Their coupling was wild and untamed, a raw expression of their desires for one another. No words were needed between them, their bodies communicating with an unspoken language that only they understood.

With each powerful thrust, he ravaged her with raw, primal intensity. The slap of his balls against her ass echoed through the room, adding to the rhythm and urgency of their passionate encounter.

Her body quivered with pleasure and desire as he took her with a ferocity she had never experienced before.

Every movement was like a symphony of lust and causing her to lose herself in the moment. This was ecstasy in its most intense form, a pure expression of their burning desire for each other.

Alder could feel the eruption building within him, a fire burning hotter and hotter until it consumed him completely. When it finally came, it felt like a supernova exploding in the depths of his being.

Without hesitation, he poured himself into her aching core, claiming her with a ferocity that transcended mere physical desire. She screamed in ecstasy, their souls merging in a fiery crescendo of pleasure that left them both trembling and spent.

With the pure bliss they experienced, they were no longer two separate beings but one entity bound together by passion and desire.

As they collapsed onto the bed, their bodies intertwined and their heartbeats slowing to a steady rhythm,

Alder knew that he had found something special with this woman. And he vowed to never let her go.

"Wow, that's quite a mighty cock you've got there," she said, her hand curling around it possessively. It was slightly firm and hot to the touch, throbbing anew with desire and strength. She admired its girth and length as she explored its every inch with her hand.

"It's yours," he growled, forcing the object even more into her tightly closed fist. She could feel its pulsating heat, growing harder and more eager for action.

With each forceful stroke of it in her hand, she could sense its power building, ready to unleash itself in another frenzy of passion and desire. The intensity of the moment was almost overwhelming as he put his hand over hers and they moved in rhythm, his eyes fasted onto hers.

"It's mine," she said as if to confirm it to herself, her grip got stronger and faster because those simple words he said were magic.

"My pussy's yours too. Claim it again" she whispered, guiding his free hand to her wet clit and they locked into a heated exchange of pleasure and control."

Together they rode the waves of passion, again and again, until the moon outside their window grew tired of watching and disappeared out of their range of vision.

They made love through the dark hours, finding new peaks to conquer with every encounter, until at last, spent and satisfied, they succumbed to the embrace of sleep, entwined in the evidence of their ardor.

The next morning, they woke up entangled in each other's arms, her soft breasts comforting to his touch. The sunlight streamed in through the windows, enveloping their naked bodies in a gentle embrace of radiance.

Alder traced his fingers over her soft skin as she stirred awake. Her eyes fluttered open and she smiled at him, knowing that this was just the beginning of their journey together.

As her hand reached down, she felt his hardened manhood, a sign of his desire for her.

With a sense of urgency, she positioned herself on top of him, eagerly spreading her slick folds to envelop him within her.

She began to move with a rhythm that matched the pounding of her heart, riding him with fierce determination while he lay beneath her, appreciating her passionate and skilled movements, his hands firmly on her hips as they swayed in perfect sync.

With a wide grin spreading across his face, he exclaimed happily, "Now that's my kind of gal!"

They spent the entire day lazing around in bed, talking about everything and nothing all at once.

It felt as though time had stopped just for them.

CHAPTER 18

*T*heir breaths were still heavy, remnants of their earlier passion hanging in the air like the delicate scent of wildflowers.

With a stretch and a playful nudge from Alder, they disentangled themselves from the cocoon of blankets.

"Stay here, I'm making us breakfast," Alder said with a determined grin, his voice a deep timbre that resonated within the rustic confines of the bedroom.

Bethany arched an eyebrow, a smirk playing on her lips as she watched him saunter to the kitchen, his muscles flexing with each step.

She wrapped herself in a sheet, her stomach growling in anticipation. The sounds of sizzling and the rich aroma of sausage soon wafted back to her, teasing her senses.

"Hope you're hungry," Aaron called out, his tone carrying the pride of a man confident in his culinary prowess.

True to his word, he presented a feast fit for a wilderness king, or rather, a queen.

Sausage, eggs, and hash browns nestled in the black iron of the dutch oven, a breakfast delight that made Bethany's mouth water.

She sat at the makeshift table, a plank of wood supported by stacks of books, and dug in with gusto.

"Wow, this is amazing," she mumbled between mouthfuls, her previous skepticism about Alder's cooking skills dissolving with each bite.

"See? Told you you'd be able to handle a mountain man's breakfast," Alder boasted, his chest puffing up slightly as he joined her in the meal.

They ate in comfortable silence, the occasional glance or brush of hands sending ripples of warmth through them.

It was Bethany who broke the quiet with a chuckle, recalling the bet she had made and lost the night of her bachelorette party.

"Looks like I lost my bachelorette party bet, but honestly," she leaned forward, her eyes glinting with mischief, "cock beats all."

Alder's laughter filled the room, a rich sound that mingled with the crackling fire in the hearth. They shared a moment of pure contentment, reveling in the unexpected connection that had blossomed between them.

"Let me clean up," Bethany offered, already gathering the plates. Her insistence was met with a playful swat from Aaron, sending him off to his office while she tackled the dishes with a song in her heart.

Moments later, after scrubbing the last pan, she made her way to his office, curious to see where he spent his hours when not engulfed in nature or, other activities.

The door creaked open to reveal walls lined with shelves, each one laden with books, a collection as vast as the forest outside.

Her gaze fell upon a series of novels, their spines identical to those she had seen in Aaron's cabin. A frown creased her brow. Why would he have these here, too?

"Alder?" she called out, unsure now as her heart began to thump erratically.

He turned his head and saw where her eyes were fixated, his usual confidence faltered under her questioning gaze. Redness crept up his neck as he realized what had caught her attention.

Bethany's brow furrowed even deeper as she tried to grasp the sudden change in atmosphere.

She had been so caught up in the blissful moments with Alder that it hadn't occurred to really delve into his personal life.

But now, with his awkward fumbling and flushed cheeks, she couldn't help but wonder what he was hiding.

"What is this all about?" she asked, her curiosity piqued. Were the two men into weird stuff?

Alder sighed and ran a hand through his hair. "I'm a writer," he admitted reluctantly.

"A writer?" Bethany repeated, surprise evident in her tone. "But I thought you were a wilderness king."

He chuckled wryly. "Yeah, that was just a little ruse I came up with to get my mind off things and focus on my writing."

Bethany's eyes widened in realization. The similarities between his books and their experience together suddenly made sense. "So... these books are based on your life?" she asked tentatively.

Alder shook his head, his expression sheepish. "Mostly from my imagination."

Bethany's heart skipped a beat as she looked at him anew. She had always been an avid reader, granted she didn't read in the genre she wrote.

The fact that Alder was a writer like her made her feel even more connected to him in a way she never thought possible.

Alder took her hand in his then, looking at her with earnest eyes. "I know you find this probably strange and maybe even a little deceitful, but it's what I do, and I'm damned good at it if I might be so bold.

She could feel the sincerity in every word he spoke and it warmed her from the inside out.

"I didn't tell you before because... well, because I was afraid and saving it for later," Alder continued, his voice wavering slightly.

Bethany studied him, searching his face for honesty. His eyes held a hint of vulnerability she hadn't seen before, and it tugged at something deep within her.

Her upset melted into a cautious curiosity, wondering how much more there was to discover about the man who had already surprised her in so many ways.

CHAPTER 19

*T*he room had been immersed in a cozy silence, punctuated only by the occasional crackle from the fireplace, when Alder's confession about his career as a romance novelist hung in the air like an exposed secret.

His heart rate ticked up a notch, his palms slightly damp as he awaited Bethany's response.

What followed was not the understanding nod he had anticipated, but an eruption of laughter from her, loud and uninhibited, ricocheting off the walls and piercing through the warmth of the moment.

Alder's brow furrowed, his puzzled expression slowly morphing into a mask of hurt.

The laughter, so unexpected and seemingly mocking, clawed at his chest, tugging at the thread of insecurity he thought he had tucked away.

Each chuckle felt like a jab, undermining the passion he poured into his writing, his art that he had just laid bare before her.

"There's no reason to mock my job," he said, his voice carrying an edge sharpened by rising anger.

The words were a defensive shield, attempting to guard the vulnerability that now felt like foolishness.

He stood tense, a statue of indignation, the warmth of the room doing nothing to thaw the chill that had swiftly descended between them.

Alder searched her eyes for a sliver of remorse, for any sign that she understood the gravity of her reaction.

"How could you be so cruel?" he asked, the question more to himself than to Bethany. It was a whisper of betrayal, the echoes of his own doubts given voice.

In his mind, the years he'd spent honing his craft seemed to unravel, thread by thread, with each peal of her laughter.

"Is it only women that are allowed to write with passion?" His words were a challenge now, heavy with implication.

Alder's gaze held hers firmly as if daring her to affirm the stereotype that men couldn't possibly weave tales of love and longing as she did.

There was a storm behind his eyes, a turbulent clash of pride and pain, waiting to see if she would pour more rain onto it or offer a much-needed shelter.

Bethany's laughter faltered as she caught the storm brewing in Alder's eyes.

A hand fluttered to her chest, an instinctive gesture of contrition.

"Oh, Alder, I, I'm so sorry," she stammered, the humor draining from her voice as she realized the hurt she had inadvertently caused. "I'm not laughing at your job, I promise you."

Alder's stance remained rigid, his defenses up, a sentinel against further ridicule. But he saw the genuine concern etching her features and allowed himself a cautious breath.

"It's just that it's such a coincidence," Bethany continued, her smile returning, but this time it was tinged with sheepishness. "You see, I write romance novels too." She bit her lip, gauging his reaction before adding, "Under a pen name too, actually."

The ice that had formed around Alder's heart cracked slightly. A pen name? Curiosity peeked through the veil of his indignation.

"Really?" He couldn't keep the skepticism entirely out of his voice, but the sharp edges were blunted by intrigue.

"Really," Bethany affirmed with a nod. "My books are on those same shelves your work graces." She laughed again, softer now, inviting him into the shared absurdity of the situation.

And just like that, they found themselves on common ground, the tension dissolving into shared confidences about their secret writerly lives.

They traded tales of sleepless nights fueled by inspiration, of characters that whispered secrets only to them. Each revelation spun a thread, weaving the fabric of a newfound camaraderie between them.

As Alder listened to Bethany confess her commitment to her craft, how she'd adored the universe he created in one of his novels during her stay at Aaron's cabin, he felt seen in a way he hadn't anticipated. "I started reading

'Throbbing Of My Heart,'" she said, her enthusiasm evident. "It's wonderful."

"Thank you," Alder replied, a flush of pride warming his cheeks. Her compliment felt like a balm to his earlier wounds.

Then, with a mischievous glint in her eyes, Bethany leaned closer. "Have you ever thought about bringing one of your chapters to life?" Her voice dipped into a sultry octave that sent a thrill down Alder's spine.

"Which chapter did you have in mind?" he asked, already knowing he'd agree to whatever she proposed.

"Chapter six," she whispered, referring to a particularly passionate scene.

"Yes," Alder said without hesitation, the word wrapped in eagerness. He reached for her hand, a spark igniting between them as their fingers intertwined.

Together, they made their way toward the bedroom, each step pulsing with the anticipation of art imitating life.

But just before crossing the threshold of the room where fiction would blend with reality, Bethany tugged at his hand, pulling him toward another detour.

"Wait," she said, her voice laced with playful urgency. They veered into the kitchen, where she retrieved a can of whipped cream from the refrigerator, a prop befitting the chapter they intended to honor.

"Hot diggity!" Alder exclaimed with a joyful shout that echoed through the air for miles.

With a shared conspiratorial grin, they continued their journey, ready to breathe life into the words they both so passionately crafted.

CHAPTER 20

*B*ethany's boots crunched on the carpet of pine needles as she followed Alder through a copse of tall aspens, their leaves trembling and whispering secrets to the mountain breeze.

Her breath misted in the cool air, and she pulled her jacket tighter around her.

The Bethany from a week ago would have balked at the thought of baiting a hook or foraging for wild herbs, but here she was now, her hands dirt-stained and her face aglow with newfound resilience.

"Watch your step over these roots," Alder called back, his voice softened by the forest's hush.

The corners of his eyes crinkled in amusement each time she narrowly avoided a stumble. He no longer had the hardened lines of a recluse, but warm creases etched by shared mirth.

As dusk painted the sky in hues of lavender and rose, they returned to the cabin, their laughter echoing off the trunks of trees, carrying away the last remnants of any awkwardness that had lingered between them.

Later, they sat side by side on rough-hewn log benches, the fire before them crackling its approval at their companionship.

The night sky unfurled above with millions of endless stars winking down at them. Bethany drew her knees up, wrapping her arms around them as she gazed into the flames.

Alder broke the silence first, his voice low and as raw as the wood he fed to the fire.

"My father brought me here when I was about ten," he began, the orange glow reflecting in his eyes. "Taught me how to read the land and pay it its due respect. He'd say, 'Nature doesn't need us, but we sure as hell need it. I never found where he's heard it first."

Listening, Bethany felt the weight of his solitude, the strength in his connection to the untamed landscape.

She saw the boy who learned from the earth, grew into the man who became one with it.

Her heart skipped when he told her of his narrow brush with death and she squeezed his hand.

"I used to think I couldn't live without the city's pulse," she found herself responding, her voice threading through the smoke that curled towards the heavens. "The buzz of people, the chaos, it was like... music, you know? But there's another kind of rhythm out here, isn't there? One that's slower, but just as alive."

They sat in companionable silence for a while longer, both lost in their own thoughts. The fire died down to embers, casting shadows across their faces.

Bethany traced the patterns of stars above with her finger, her mind drifting back to the city she had left behind.

She spoke of her life, of the never-ending race on asphalt tracks, the cacophony of sirens and chatter that never truly let her mind rest.

There was vulnerability in her admission, an openness that the Bethany of before, wrapped up in urban armor, would never have shown.

Alder listened intently, his gaze unwavering as she spoke. He could see the weight lifted off her shoulders with each word she shared. And when she finally fell silent, he reached out and took her hand in his.

"You don't have to go back," he said softly. "Not if you don't want to."

Bethany's brow furrowed in confusion. "What do you mean?"

"I mean...you found something here," Alder said, gesturing to the surrounding forest. "Something that called to you and made you stay." He paused, his eyes searching hers for understanding. "You can keep it with you always."

A small smile tugged at Bethany's lips as she realized what he was saying. She didn't have to leave this peaceful haven behind. She could take it with her wherever she went.

"Thank you," she whispered earnestly, but her mind was torn.

They sat there for a few moments longer before Alder stood up and offered his hand to help Bethany up as well.

"I think it's time we turn in for the night," he said, giving her a warm smile.

They made love long into the night and Bethany felt a sense of contentment wash over her. For once in a long time, she felt truly at peace.

The revelation hung in the space between them, as she fell asleep, mingling with the scent of pine and woodsmoke.

She turned to Alder, his profile etched against the flickering light, and in his presence, she found an unexpected sanctuary.

Neither of them spoke of tomorrow, of the decisions that loomed like distant peaks.

For now, it was enough to share the warmth and the silent understanding that something within them both had irreversibly shifted.

CHAPTER 21

*B*ethany awoke to the soft glow of dawn caressing the rustic contours of Alder's cabin.

For a fleeting moment, the simplicity of mountain living enveloped her, offering a peace she hadn't known among the steel and glass spires of her former life.

She watched Alder, still asleep, his chest rising and falling with a rhythm that echoed the steadiness of the hills themselves.

Over mugs of black coffee, as golden rays spilled over the porch, they spoke little of the day ahead.

Their conversations had crafted a colorful mosaic of shared experiences over the short amount of time they'd spent together.

However, as they confronted the weighty decision hanging over them that morning, words felt insufficient against the backdrop of their contemplation.

"Maybe it's just the mountains," Bethany finally said, breaking the silence, "but I can't imagine not waking up to all of this." Her gaze swept the horizon, lingering on the forests that had slowly begun to feel like home.

Alder nodded, his eyes mirroring the deep connection he felt for the lands. "I've spent years carving out a life here," he admitted. "The thought of leaving..." His voice trailed off, unfinished, but the sentiment hung heavy in the air.

Their ease with one another was undeniable. Laughter came quickly, touches lingered, and glances held warmth that neither had anticipated.

Yet the question of where they would live turned into an invisible chasm, growing wider with each passing day.

As the week neared its end, the line between teacher and student blurred into something more profound. Bethany, once frustrated with the mountain challenges, found herself strangely attached to the serenity of the place. Alder, in turn, discovered a warmth within him that he hadn't felt in years.

Their banter had transformed into a playful exchange of affection. Bethany, who once complained about the rustic life, now found comfort in the simplicity of it all.

Intimate moments unfolded naturally, shared glances lingering a moment longer, and subtle touches speaking volumes.

Bethany took long walks by herself sometimes, her feet tracing paths through the wilderness, while her mind wandered back to the city. The thought of abandoning her life, the pace of urban existence wasn't an easy thing to consider.

Could she leave behind the harsh, unyielding concrete

for the soft, fertile soil? Could she exchange the constant blare of sirens for the soothing symphony of bird calls?

Alder watched her grapple with the decision, his own heart leaden at the idea of parting ways.

He could feel the weight of his guilt like a heavy cloak, suffocating him as he wanted nothing more than to beg her to stay and join him in his secluded paradise.

The thought of asking her to give up everything for him, however, was like a blade twisting in his gut, tearing him apart with self-loathing and doubt.

He feared her potential blame, as it had destroyed his relationship once before. Yet, he couldn't bear the thought of losing her. He was torn between wanting to protect himself and wanting to salvage their love.

Yes, I know I'm in love with Bethany.

At the end of the week which approached much too quickly for both of them, with bags packed and the car idling outside, they stood facing each other, the weight of unmade choices pressing down upon them. Their hands met, fingers intertwining with a quiet desperation.

Bethany's words were a desperate whisper, barely audible above the howling wind and rustling leaves. "We need more time," she pleaded, her voice strained with fear and urgency.

Alder squeezed her hand, his eyes searching hers for answers neither could find. "I know," he replied, the furrows in his brow deepening. "I know."

Please stay.

They stood there, the morning chill wrapping around them, two souls caught between worlds, worrying about a future that was as uncertain as the shifting mountain shadows.

CHAPTER 22

$\mathcal{T}$he last light of the sun kissed the winding road, illuminating it softly as Bethany's car gracefully navigated each curve.

She gripped the steering wheel tighter, her knuckles turning white as she fought the urge to turn around and race back to Alder.

She knew they both needed time to reflect on the whirlwind of emotions that had engulfed them in the mountains so she resisted.

"Time and distance," she muttered to herself, trying to convince her heart to listen to reason. As the town came into view, Bethany's phone buzzed with a message from Emily, Aaron's newlywed wife.

"Can't wait to catch up! See you soon!" The text brimmed with excitement, a contagious enthusiasm that coaxed a smile onto Bethany's lips.

"Likewise!" she replied, her mind momentarily distracted from the ache of missing Alder.

Upon arriving at the quaint café, Bethany was immediately enveloped in a tight hug by the glowing bride, still riding the high of her honeymoon.

They settled into a cozy booth, surrounded by the soft chatter of fellow patrons.

"Tell me everything!" Emily gushed, her eyes sparkling with curiosity.

"First, you have to tell me about your amazing honeymoon!"

As Emily recounted tales of romantic strolls on moonlit beaches and candlelit dinners, Bethany couldn't help but become lost in thoughts of Alder.

She found herself comparing the tender moments she shared with him among the rugged mountain peaks to Emily's idyllic honeymoon.

"Alright, your turn!" Emily prodded, noticing Bethany's faraway gaze. "I can see it in your eyes, something happened between you and Alder."

"Ah, well..." Bethany hesitated, her laughter attempting to dismiss the matter. "We had a nice time, nothing too special," she added, though her cheeks flushed with a warmth that contradicted her casual tone. It was evident that there was more to her experience than she was willing to admit.

"Come on," Emily urged, her eyes narrowing, "you're not fooling anyone. I remember that same look in my eyes when I first met Aaron."

"Alright, alright!" Bethany relented. "Yes, something happened between us. And I think. No, I know I'm in love with him." The words tumbled out in a breathless whisper, her heart pounding in her chest.

"Really?" Emily's face lit up with genuine happiness for

her friend. "I'm so thrilled for you! Alder is an amazing man. You two deserve each other."

"Thanks, Em," Bethany smiled warmly, feeling the weight of her secret lifted from her shoulders.

"Here's an idea," Emily suggested after hearing of the dilemma. "Why not take turns living at each other's places while you figure out where to settle down?"

Bethany's eyes widened, her mind racing with possibilities. "Duh! Why didn't we think of that? It's perfect! I'll talk to Alder about it right away!" She pulled out her phone and sent a quick message to Alder, proposing the idea.

"Sounds wonderful," came his eager response. "Come back to the mountains as soon as you can or let me know when I can come visit you as soon as you get back home."

The decision lifted a weight off her shoulders.

CHAPTER 23

*F*ive months had passed since Bethany and Alder had come up with the idea to take turns living at each other's places.

Between them, they were racking up many frequent flier miles.

At first, it seemed like the perfect solution because they were able to spend time together and explore each other's worlds without fully committing to one location.

But, as time went on, Bethany found herself longing for the mountains more and more.

The city that she had once loved now felt suffocating and overwhelming. How quickly life changed for them!

The constant noise of construction, the crowded subways during rush hour, and the never-ending hustle and bustle started to grate on her nerves.

Bethany missed the peacefulness of the mountains, the crisp air, and the simple way of life.

She missed waking up to the sound of birds chirping instead of car horns blaring.

She even found herself missing Alder's cabin, despite its lack of modern amenities, and that was saying a lot.

It wasn't just about missing Alder anymore, although she certainly did.

It was about realizing that she had outgrown the city lifestyle and yearned for a quieter, simpler life in the mountains with him.

A passing bus had soaked her, splashing muddy water onto her as she walked down the street during one particularly frustrating day in the city.

Bethany made her decision then. She no longer wanted to do the back-and-forth thing anymore.

She wanted to live with Alder full-time. All the little things that had been bothering her brought her to the final decision.

Without hesitation, she called him immediately and proposed the idea of her moving. To her delight, he eagerly agreed.

"I've been thinking about it too," he admitted, "I miss you terribly when you're not here."

Shortly thereafter, Bethany packed up hers, and, his things that he'd left when he'd made the journey and moved states, to live in Alder's lodge permanently.

It wasn't a big adjustment as most of her belongings were still in boxes from their previous arrangement. It felt different then though. Like she was finally home.

The town below became a nice middle ground for them. If Bethany ever started to feel isolated or missed the city, Alder would suggest a visit to the local farmers' market or a day trip to the urban areas nearby.

When he felt the need for a bit of solitude in the

mountains, she would happily give him the space he needed, knowing their bond was strong enough to withstand any distance.

Emily was close and, and she was pregnant, Bethany loved helping her. She couldn't believe how much her best friend glowed. She'd been a beautiful bride and would be an excellent mother.

The first night after they had fully moved her in, Bethany and Alder stood at the edge of their property, gazing out at the breathtaking view of the mountains in front of them.

"I can't believe we get to wake up to this every day," Bethany breathed, her hand intertwined with Alder's.

"It's all thanks to you," Alder said, pulling her close. "If you hadn't agreed to live up here with me, I would still be alone in this beautiful but lonely place."

"Hey now," Bethany playfully swatted his chest. "I think I got the better end of this deal!" They both laughed, enjoying their playful banter.

As if on cue, a gentle breeze blew through the trees surrounding them, carrying with it the sweet melody of a bird's song.

"This is our home now," Alder said softly.

"Our home," Bethany repeated, feeling her heart swell with love for him and their new life together.

Together they explored every inch of their property, marveling at the natural beauty surrounding them.

They discovered hidden streams and waterfalls close by that they would spend hours sitting by, listening to the soothing sounds of nature.

They hiked through thick forests, coming across all kinds of wildlife that called the mountains home.

But most importantly, they spent countless hours simply being together.

Whether it was cuddled up on the couch reading books or cooking dinner together in their cozy kitchen, they cherished every moment spent in each other's company.

With the unfamiliar sights and sounds of her new surroundings, Bethany's books took on a new depth.

They became a reflection of her evolving state of being, each page infused with the energy and excitement of her success.

As she delved deeper into the stories, she found herself soaring to new heights alongside her characters, propelled by the thrill of adventure and growth.

The pages practically crackled with electricity as her imagination exploded within the pages, intertwining with her newfound confidence.

With each turn of the page, Bethany felt herself becoming more and more intertwined with her own story, both in and out of the book.

Their love only grew stronger with each passing day

as they learned more about each other and carved out a life for themselves in this remote mountain paradise.

As winter approached and snow covered their land, they snuggled by the fireplace and watched as white flakes fell outside their window.

When spring arrived and flowers bloomed all around them, Bethany knew without a doubt that she had found her forever home and her forever love in Alder.

Their story had come full circle and they still couldn't get enough of each other.

EPILOGUE

BETHANY - SEVEN YEARS LATER

*B*ethany stood on the porch of their mountain home, a steaming mug of coffee warming her hands despite the chill in the air.

She inhaled deeply, the scent of pine and earth mingling with the crispness of the approaching dawn.

Her gaze wandered to the playground they had built for their son, now dotted with early morning dew, and a smile curled her lips as she thought about how he would be clambering over it in just a few hours.

"Time really does fly," she murmured to herself, reflecting on the seven years that seemed to have passed in the blink of an eye.

Life up here, isolated from the hustle of the city, had granted a different perspective on time. It was slower, richer, filled with quiet moments and the laughter of their three-year-old echoing off the mountains.

She glanced back at the lodge, sturdy and warm, and made from Alder's craftsmanship and the life they'd built together since that fateful day.

A surge of gratitude washed over her as she remembered their wedding, vows exchanged at the same ranch that had witnessed Aaron's own union.

The memory was vivid, draped in golden sunlight and the vibrant hues of wildflowers that had surrounded them, an amazing experience etched into her heart.

A rustle in the trees announced the arrival of Aaron, his familiar figure emerging from the path that led to his own cabin, a stone's throw away.

His wife and her best friend, Emily, followed, one child nestled in her arms and another tugging eagerly at her hand, their faces alight with the thrill of another day of adventure in the wilderness.

Bethany's son would have playmates today, cousins as they called themselves, to share in the joy and innocence of a childhood amidst nature's grandeur.

"Morning, Beth!" Aaron called out, his voice carrying through the still air. "Ready for some more mountain magic?"

"Always,I'll pop in soon as you're settled in," she answered with a laugh, waving to them.

As the children squealed and darted toward the playground, she couldn't help but muse on the prospect of this becoming more than a frequent getaway for them. Perhaps one day, they too would succumb to the call of the mountains and settle here permanently.

Bethany sipped her coffee and allowed her mind to drift back to the decision that had started it all. A crazy bet, lost on purpose or perhaps by destiny's design, which had guided her footsteps to this very spot, to Alder, to a love that felt as enduring as the peaks that cradled their home.

She raised her cup in a silent toast to fate and to the beautiful, winding journey that had brought her here.

EPILOGUE

ALDER

The crisp, morning air bit at Alder's cheeks as he lifted his son onto his shoulders, the child's laughter mingling with the rustle of fallen leaves underfoot.

They were ascending the familiar trail up the mountain back to their home, a path that held imprints of Alder's own childhood adventures.

With each step, his heart swelled with a heady mix of nostalgia and pride as he watched his little boy's eyes widen with every new discovery, from scampering chipmunks to the colorful birds that flitted from tree to tree.

"Look, Daddy! An eagle!" His son's excited shout drew Alder's gaze upward, where the majestic bird soared against the backdrop of the azure sky.

"Exactly like you, kiddo, free and fearless," Alder said with a chuckle, patting his sons chubby legs.

When they reached a clearing, Alder set his son down gently, watching him race towards a cluster of wildflowers.

The mountain had always been his home, and sharing it with his son felt like an unspoken rite of passage, a silent nod to his own father who had once guided him through these very woods.

Later, back at their cozy home and his son having rushed off to join Aaron's kids, Alder observed Bethany in her element.

Her office was a mirror of her mind: organized, vibrant, and brimming with creativity.

She was in the zone, her fingers dancing across the keyboard, her focus absolute, even with the occasional interruptions for spontaneous story brainstorming sessions between them.

He often marveled at how she cold handle a hundred different things at once without breaking a sweat.

Their literary worlds often overlapped, two sides of the coin intertwining just as their lives had.

He leaned against the doorframe, a contented sigh escaping him. Together, they had built a life that allowed them to flourish not only as parents and partners but also as individuals with successful careers.

The coalition of their relationship extended into their writing, each one's success fueling the other's.

Alder's thoughts drifted to the previous night, the memories vivid enough to elicit a physical response.

Bethany was passion incarnate, a woman who matched his intensity in every facet of their life together.

He grinned, acknowledging the surge of desire that reminded him just how much she still affected him.

"Thinking about your next chapter?" Bethany called

out, her perceptive eyes meeting his as she sensed his presence.

"Something like that," he replied with a wry smile, his innuendo hanging in the air like the delicate perfume of her laughter.

"Insatiable," Bethany's voice was thick with desire as her husband approached, his eyes dark with hunger.

Their son was safely occupied with their friends' children, giving them the freedom to indulge in each other without any interruptions.

With a quick turn of her head, Bethany reached for Alder's pants, unzipping them to free his already stiff and oozing cock.

She wasted no time in taking him into her mouth, delighted by his gruff moans and the way his hand grabbed the back of her head and settled himself on the edge of her desk.

She hummed in pleasure as she deepened the depth, savoring the familiar taste of him.

"You're my kind of gal," he muttered as he ground himself to her eager mouth, his fingers tangling in her hair as she brought him closer to the edge.

Bethany grinned mischievously as she pulled away, leading him towards their bedroom.

Her body ached for his touch, craving the sensation of being consumed by him.

They moved together in perfect rhythm and she always surrendered herself fully to the pleasure and ecstasy coursing through her veins.

His presence inside her was intoxicating, drowning

out all else as they became one in a fiery inferno of passion.

Their lovemaking had evolved to be an art form, one they had perfected over years of practice and love.

In between breathless kisses and sultry caresses, Alder felt a sense of contentment.

This was their haven, a place where they could be completely themselves without any pretense or expectations from the outside world.

Afterward, they lay tangled after their passionate release, Bethany traced patterns on his chest with her fingers while he played idly with strands of her hair.

They were both content to bask in each other's presence before reality came knocking again.

"We should probably get back to work," Alder said with a regretful sigh.

Bethany chuckled and nodded in agreement before snuggling closer to him.

As much as she loved writing and all it entailed, plot twists, character development, and endless revisions, moments like these reminded her that there was more to life than just their stories.

"How about one more quickie instead?" she mumbled into his chest.

"Who's insatiable again?" he asked once more with a small laugh as he slid himself inside her in one swift movement that left her gasping.

Indeed, he knew without a doubt that he was a man graced with fortune far beyond the pages of any bestseller.

THANK YOU

Thank you so much for your purchase. I appreciate it very much.

MAKE MY DAY

If you enjoyed the book, you can leave a review on whatever platform you purchased it from, and **especially on my website**.

Reviews are crucial for indie authors like me who don't have powerhouse publishing companies behind them.

Just look for the WRITE A CUSTOMER REVIEW link. Your review will help with exposure to others who might enjoy the same.

Reading your kind reviews brightens my day and pushes me to be even better. Please be sure to let me know what you loved most about this book.

Join my newsletter to stay updated on new book releases and bonuses. Simply scan the QR code for the website.

THANK YOU

You've glimpsed Amber and Fletch in this story. You can read their story in this book.

Protected by the Rancher

Will the rancher rope the woman in peril that he rescued?

Amber:

A year ago, having escaped my past and now living in this quaint town far, far away. Now, he's found me, and my new life is shattered. Finding myself in a dangerous situation, all seemed to be lost until my rancher came to the rescue. Now safely ensconced and guarded by him, I am finally starting to relax.

Then, Axel, my bad-to-the-bone ex turns up again like a bad penny.

Fletch:

Happy to remain a bachelor, I am content with running my ranch. Then I meet Amber, a beautiful woman with a secret past. Rescuing and protecting her was a no-brainer, and not just because I crave her curvy body.

Can he save her in time once more?

If you love the age gap and woman in peril tropes, then you'll love Amber and Fletch in Protected by the Rancher.

There's NO cheating and NO cliffhangers. Sweet, sexy HEA guaranteed.

https://vestaromero.com/product/protected-by-the-rancher/

Mountain Man's Melody is a satisfying insta-love romance that unfolds amidst the unpredictable beauty of Gable's mountain retreat. Pilot Amelia, thrust into a storm, finds herself in the rugged seclusion that becomes the backdrop for an unforgettable love story.

In this swoon-worthy tale, Amelia and Gable's journey begins with sparks flying, where grumpy meets sunshine and laughter echoes through their intimate moments. As they navigate the raging emotions, shared glances, and the warmth of a crackling fireplace, their love story blooms against all odds.

Join the steamy fun as this woman breaks down the mountain man's defenses, revealing that the most enchanting melodies are discovered in the unlikeliest places.

Are you ready for a desire-filled read that unfolds when you least expect it? Mountain Man's Melody is filled with passion and warmth that will keep you hooked from beginning to end.

https://vestaromero.com/product/mountain-mans-melody/

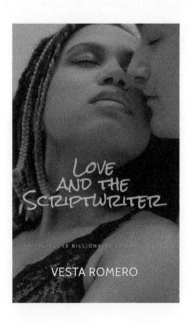

In a world of Hollywood glamour and glittering dreams, one curvy scriptwriter's journey to love will make you swoon. As she navigates the chaos of movie-making, little does she know that her heart's leading role is to be played by an unexpected, charming extra.

Sparks ignited on set as they fell into a whirlwind romance faster than any Hollywood plot twist she could have come up with. But when the truth behind her leading man's identity is revealed, she's left feeling like a pawn in a billion-dollar game.

Theirs is a rollercoaster ride through Tinseltown, where love transcends appearances and trust is reborn. Drama, passion, and redemption are plentiful as Serena, the heroine, and her billionaire producer find their way back to love beneath the Hollywood lights.

This hot and sizzling romance defies stereotypes, proving that love knows no bounds and that curvy is beautiful and oh-so-hot. You don't miss this spicy romance where chaos and chance conspire to create a Hollywood ending worth waiting for.

https://vestaromero.com/product/love-and-the-scriptwriter-ebook/

A curvy girl love story. Can these two polar opposites find love and make it work?

Cam:

It was supposed to be another dull day on the bunny slopes until this curvaceous and extremely sexy woman turns up just in time to turn my life upside down. Playing nurse has never felt so good.

Misty:

I'm a city girl at heart, a fish out of the water at this resort. I only agreed to come at the insistence of my best friend. Now, she can't make it and I'm stuck. All l want is the freebies that come with the suite. An impulsive decision to take a ski lesson with the hot instructor lands me on my bum and has me questioning everything l ever believed.

https://vestaromero.com/product/love-and-the-ski-instructor/

Can this grumpy billionaire and feisty pharmacist discover the love that neither one knew they wanted?

Carmen:

All I wanted to do after my long shift was to go home and ride out the storm like everyone else. A simple error has me delivering much-needed medication to the sexy and prickly billionaire that came in earlier that evening. I probably could have found someone else to do it, but I longed to see him once more.

Walter:

I screwed up my first meeting with the gorgeous redheaded woman behind the counter. Serendipity brings her to my doorstep and I couldn't be happier at the chance to start fresh. If she'll let me.

Sparks fly when the two are forced to spend time together in a snowstorm. One night might be all it takes for these opposites to attract but can they survive his mother's meddling?

If you enjoy the billionaire and opposite attraction tropes, you'll love The Billionaire's Redhead. No cheating or cliffhanger, only short and steamy romance.

https://vestaromero.com/product/the-billionaires-redhead/

Vesta's books are also widely available on your favorite buying platform if that is your preference. She appreciates your support by buying direct.

ABOUT THE AUTHOR

Vesta Romero writes love stories about curvy women and the men who love them.

She lives in Spain with her husband and Texas born dog. When not writing smutty books, she enjoys margaritas and action movies. She'd love to hear from her readers; reach her on Tik-Tok, Twitter or Instagram.

To stay updated on new releases and specials, join her newsletter via the website.

Vestaromero

Vesta's stories are short, sweet, and steamy with guaranteed HEA.

Milton Keynes UK
Ingram Content Group UK Ltd.
UKHW010626290424
441924UK00001B/43